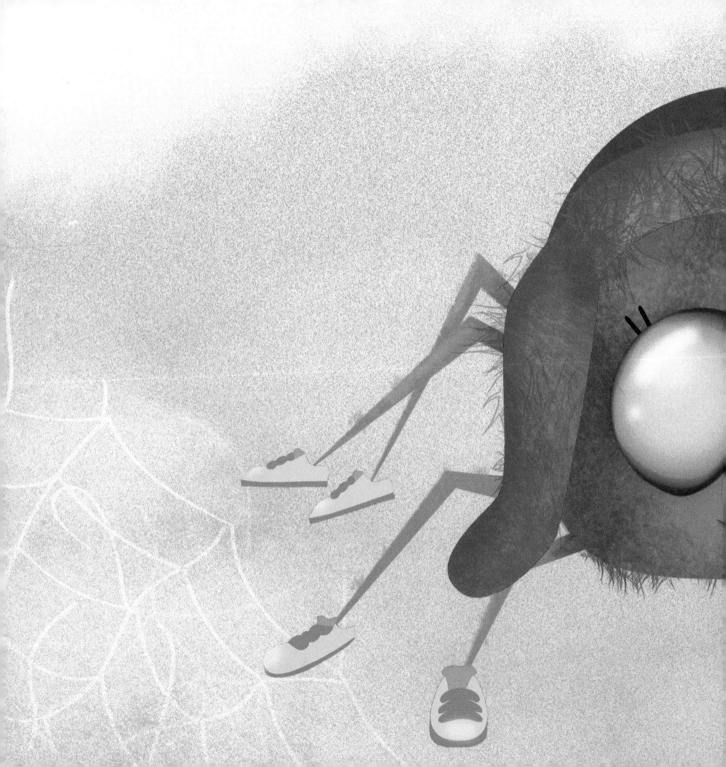

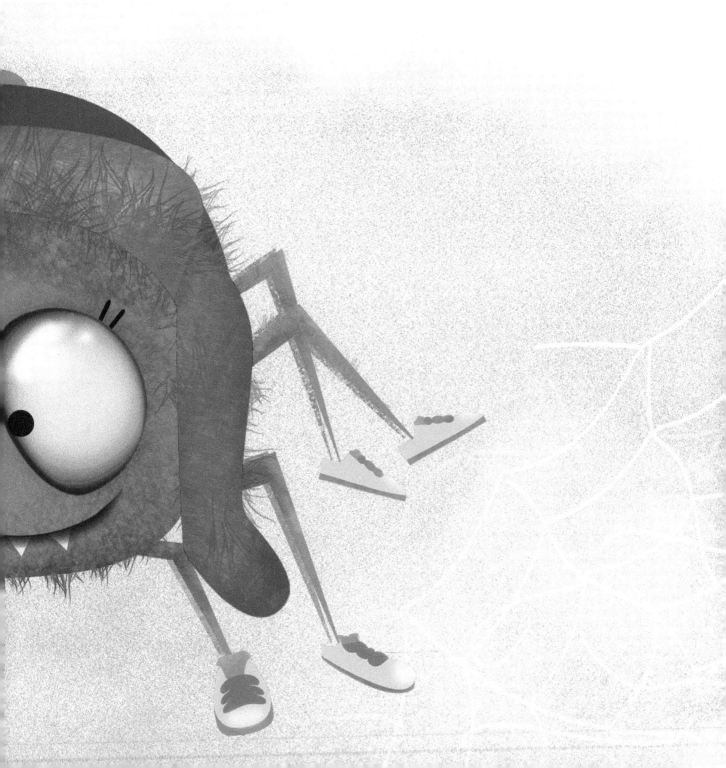

This book is given with love

To: _____

From: _____

This book is for my mother,
Martha is her name.
Without her kind encouragement,
Life wouldn't be the same!

She created Salaperantha,
Now this book is my decree.
To honor all her talent,
And for all the world to see.

I want her to remember,
That in every simple way,
Her creative genius inspires me,
Every single day.

I love you, mom!

For all inquiries, please contact us at:

info@puppysmiles.org

To see more of our books, visit us at:

www.PuppyDogsAndIceCream.com

Salaperantha
What's Your Special Skill?

Written by Jacqueline Khoenle

Illustrations by Andrea Aliani

There was a spider, whose given name, was simply Salaperantha,
Not Sarah, Sasha, Sofie, Sibyl, Sally, or Samantha.
She lived on a giant farm, in a peaceful, country town,
With Chromius, the clever cat, and the farmer, Mr. Brown.

She always spun her sturdy webs of shiny, shimmering silk,

Above the brown, humongous cows that daily gave the milk.

Silently hanging from her webs, hour after hour,

Thinking of her tasty prey, that she would soon devour.

She would spin all day long, above her furry friends,

The cows, goats, donkeys, sheep, and even cackling hens.

The horses, pigs, ducks, and the many fluffy rabbits,

The turkeys, emus, and little calves with all their crazy habits.

The ducks and hens laid the eggs, the mules helped harvest wheat,

But others offered different things you simply could not eat.

The horses gave so many rides, the goats would eat the weeds,

All the animals worked on the farm, fulfilling every need.

But Salaperantha wanted to achieve such great things, too,

She wished she could discover what exactly she could do.

For all her friends had purposes and tasks they could complete,

She could not stop believing that she just could not compete.

She asked herself so often, "But what could be my task?"

She looked amongst her barn friends, finding someone she could ask.

Chromius, the kitty, had so many great degrees,

He worked so hard, did his best, and earned them all with ease.

Mr. Brown, the farmer, was witty and so smart.

He educated Chromius, right from the very start.

The kitty's main degree was displayed upon a shelf,

And written very clearly, "Keep believing in yourself!"

Chromius was oh so wise and slowly he explained,

Yet after they had chatted, Salaperantha soon exclaimed,

"But I'm a simple spider and a wacky one at that!

I'm cross-eyed, wear bright sneakers and a furry bomber's hat."

Chromius continued, "Life is sometimes just so tough.

Bad things will surely happen, and you'll think you've had enough.

But you need to just keep trying and change the way you think.

Everyone has a special skill!" Then he gave a heartfelt wink.

But there had to be much more to this simple way of life.

Though she knew it was much better than one filled with so much strife.

She needed something different, and a rest that she could take,

She was tired of spinning only webs and longed to take a break.

Salaperantha then retreated directly to the mill,
It was peaceful and so quiet and it's where she could just chill.
Mrs. Mouse also lived there with six little ones in tow,
The days were peaceful and so calm, they seemed to pass so slow.

They all lived together for months and months on end.
Salaperantha and Mrs. Mouse soon became the best of friends.
But she still wanted badly to achieve something great,
To be SO good at something, she simply couldn't wait!

Salaperantha did like living with all the little mice.

But she missed her cat friend, Chromius, and all his wise advice.

The mill was always quiet, one couldn't hear a stir.

Then one day, from high above, a rumbling did occur!

In the barn, the dogs were barking, and the cows were mooing,

Outside the sky grew very dark, a massive storm was brewing!

Chromius, the cat, who was as brilliant as a fox,

Ran to hide, at lightning speed, into a hefty box!

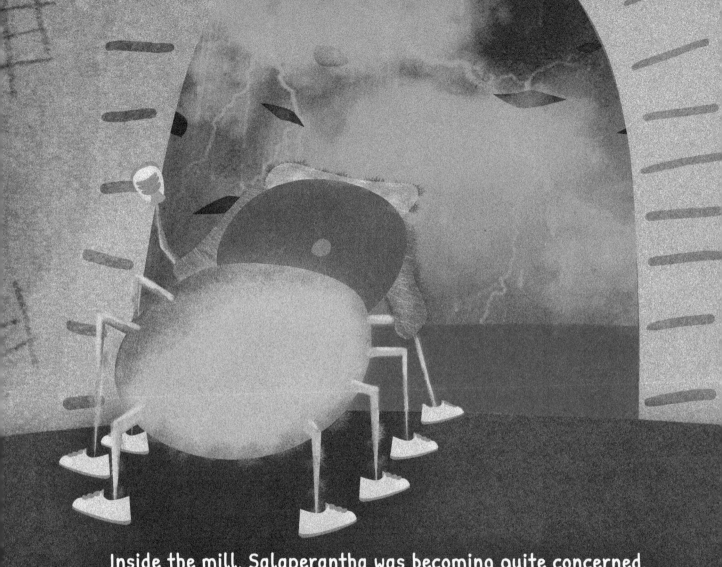

Inside the mill, Salaperantha was becoming quite concerned,
She knew these storms were scary, in the past, as she had learned.
She knew the webs she spun at home, would quiver and would shake,
But they stayed strong, no matter what, and simply wouldn't break!

Safe on her web she would survive the very scary storms.

And she'd spin more webs, right after, which was always just the norm.

But this storm was very different, it was frightful and severe,

The thunder kept on booming, it filled everyone with fear.

There was a roaring river which flowed beside the mill,

It was lined with splendid trees and twisted down the hill.

A storm like this would surely cause the aging mill to flood,

It would soon be filled with many things like pebbles, sticks, and mud.

Salaperantha was so worried, not knowing what to do,
She knew a plan was needed but she didn't have a clue.
All who lived inside the mill could run straight towards the barn,
Across the rugged, wooden bridge without a chance of harm.

But the old, wooden bridge began to quickly bend and sway,

And without warning, broke in half, and swiftly washed away.

The rain was still so heavy, and the wind still blew so hard,

The lightning was still striking, and the sky was still so dark!

Salaperantha also knew if the old mill was destroyed,

It would be a huge disaster, but maybe one they could avoid.

"If we made it to the barn, then we'd soon all be okay.

But how do we cross the river since the bridge has washed away?"

Mrs. Mouse was squealing, and her children worried, too.
Salaperantha kept on thinking, "Just what are we to do?"
Then suddenly she remembered, what Chromius had said.
"Everyone has a special skill", she then felt brave instead.

She knew she could spin webs, ones that didn't break.
She'd spin across the river, a bridge her web would make.
Mrs. Mouse was frightened, then let out a mighty yelp,
But Salaperantha said, "Don't worry, I think that I can help!"

Salaperantha said to Mrs. Mouse, "Just follow me!
Run down to the river and then wait beneath a tree."
Mrs. Mouse then grabbed her babies and ran out of the mill,
Across a stormy meadow and down a mighty hill.

Salaperantha reached the river; the mice had reached a tree,
The storm was still so frightening, and the grass was slippery.
She started to create her web to finally bridge the river,
Battling against the winds that made her start to shiver.

Without a thought, she spun a web, continuing to fight,
Back and forth, across the rocks, she spun with all her might.
And though she was completely soaked, no other task she'd choose,
For, after all, this able spider wore a hat and shoes.

Mrs. Mouse and her little ones now had to get across,

They were so very worried, and were simply at a loss.

But Salaperantha thought that she could help with this one, too.

She hatched a plan for them to cross...she knew just what to do!

"Mrs. Mouse, hop on my back, I'll carry you across!

And your sweet, tiny babies will be saved at any cost.

Your infants, you have six of them, my legs, well, I have eight.

Have each hang onto one of them! Come quick, we mustn't wait!"

And as they dashed across the web, there surely was no doubt,

With all the mice now hanging on, Salaperantha was worn out!

But as she ran through lightning strikes, her courage was her guide,

They landed soon on soggy ground; they'd reached the other side!

They made it across the river but could not celebrate,

They had to run back toward the barn, they simply couldn't wait.

Salaperantha ran very fast so they would all survive,

Through lightning, rain, and awful winds, they finally arrived!

And as they stood, no longer scared, the barn doors opened wide,

The animals celebrated, and Salaperantha beamed with pride.

Mrs. Mouse and her little ones were crying happy tears,

Salaperantha now stood proudly, enjoying all the cheers!

Chromius, the smart, old cat had many things to say,

The barn fell silent as he spoke while he sat upon the hay.

He said he knew THIS spider, with her grand eight-legged charm,

Would discover strength inside herself and make it to the barn.

She used her talents and her heart, but never realized,

That doing just what she does best, held such a great surprise.

She learned our skills can always be used to help each other out,

And that being proud of your own skills is what life is all about.

So, if you spin webs, wear a hat, and have eight legs or just two,

Remember to always do your best and simply just be YOU!

Claim your FREE Gift!

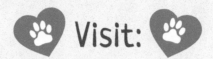 Visit:

PDICBOOKS.COM/GIFT

Thank you for purchasing

Salaperantha

and welcome to the Puppy Dogs & Ice Cream family.
We're certain you're going to love the little gift
we've prepared for you at the website above.

Meet the Author

Jacqueline Khoenle has never written a book until now! After graduating from Kent State University in 1993 with a BS in Business Administration, she moved out of her parent's house to start a career.

During that time, she would still partake in her true passions; art and creative writing. Not able to ignore her passions, she decided to write a children's book about a wacky spider named Salaperantha.

The character was created by the real artist in the family, her mother, Martha. Consequently, the book was presented to her mother as a gift on her 83rd birthday!

When she isn't writing, Jacqueline can be seen at the gym, perusing multiple home design websites, watching British TV shows, and holding great conversations with her two, "terrible" kitties. Fueled by Cheetos and Ranch dressing, she plans to write more books in the future!

Meet The Illustrator

Andrea Aliani is a book illustrator and graphic designer from Buenos Aires, Argentina. Upon graduating from the University of Buenos Aires, she continued her illustrating and designing career in Spain. Her intention to stay for only one summer turned into a five-year adventure! While there, she not only cultivated her career but met her future husband.

Since returning to Argentina, she continues to work from her charming home, which was built in 1914. After lovingly transforming the house, she can only describe it as a "magical place". When she's not creating her whimsical characters, she can be seen wrangling her son and two precious pups, Muna and Cloe. She can be contacted through her website, estudiopigmenta.com.

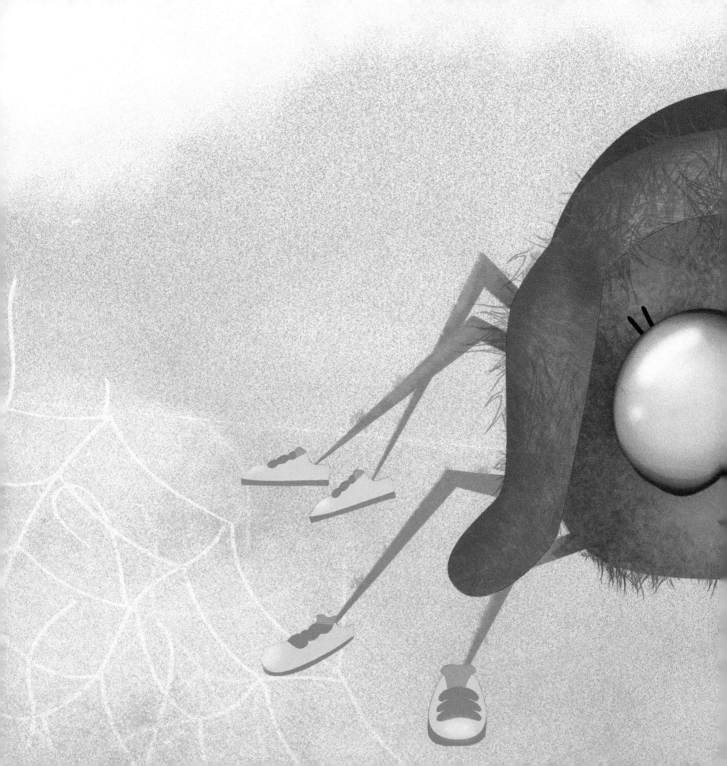

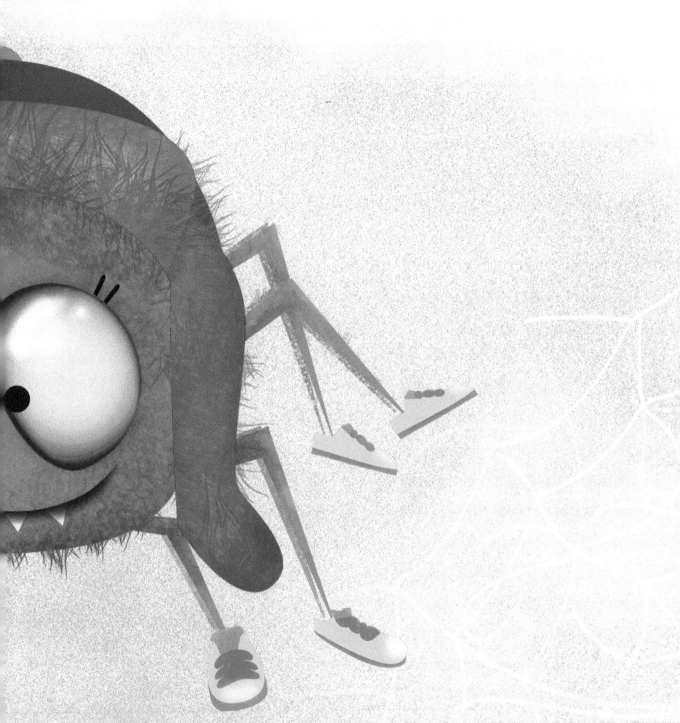

CPSIA information can be obtained
at www.ICGtesting.com
Printed in the USA
BVHW020215221122
652494BV00026B/223